Midnight Mayhem
Volume1

table of Contents

1,Portraits

I remember the exact day I received the portrait in the mail and the strange note that came with it. It was a portrait of a very old man and two women with no heads and the note that said, just for you, a friend.

I remember wondering who could of sent me such a strange gruesome thing, I was new in town and didn't know a soul. And none of my friends would have done that too me. I was almost tempted to throw it away but had the strange feeling I shouldn't. Besides the strange phone calls threatened me with a very gruesome death if I did.

Hell, I couldn't even go to the police they threatened me about that too, I was stuck between a rock and a hard place . Damned if I did and damned if I didn't, I didn't know what to do and it scared me.

Plus, I absolutely hated the portrait, it seemed that no matter what I did with it and where I hid it, the damn thing always appeared back above my fireplace. I swore that the thing was possessed, and I was afraid I was going to be too if I kept it. Plus, every time it reappeared there were small subtle changes to it. Now there were specks of splattered blood dripping from the necks of the headless women, and it wasn't paint, it was the real thing.

How that came to be, was beyond me, for I had never showed it to a single living soul. And if that wasn't bad enough, I was starting to hear women's voices that came from everywhere but nowhere. Pitifully , terrifying crying voices. Voices of the dead, begging me to help them. " Help us Cara please help us, set us free, before it's too late."

But how could I possibly do that it was just a painting of a portrait, at least that's what I tried to tell myself. But deep inside I knew it was much more sinister than that. For even the expression on the old man's face had changed, what was once gentle and benign was becoming more and more twisted and evil as he mocked me, from the fireplace wall.

I couldn't even track down who had sent it to me in the first place, for there had been no post mark or address , it had simply been wrapped in plain brown paper. I even had the sickening feeling if I were to look for fingerprints there would be none...

A thought that chilled me to the core. Usually, I enjoyed spooky mysteries, but I wasn't enjoying this one at all, as a matter of fact I found it terrifying, for the portrait was changing again before my very eyes. A fourth form seemed to be taking shape a form more terrifying than the rest and I seemed to recognize this one but how could that possibly be.

As I looked at it I realized the fourth form was me, I could barely get out a scream as the feel of cold steel, hit me full force, as I looked up I saw the old man in the portrait had swung the cold cruel blade, as I fell to the floor, I realized that whoever had sent this had intended for this to happen and there wasn't a damn thing I could do about it as my blood gurgled and I took my last dying breath.

2,Gramma

My name is Anna, and my gramma Hannah is not your usual gramma, she loves all things spooky and scary and thinks I should too, you can tell from the creepy packages she keeps sending me. And though I've told her I don't like the packages, she keeps sending them and they just keep getting creepier and creepier, especially this newest one.

It completely unnerved me and was sure to give me nightmares. Nightmares I wouldn't   get over. Though I collect dolls, I did not like this one, it ran with no batteries, and no matter what I did with it. It kept coming back in the same package with Grammas name on it.

And every time I called her about it ,she said she didn't do it and had no idea what I was talking about. And to make matters worse the thing started talking even without batteries. " Anna, don't you love me?" It would ask. " I love you if you don't love me, I'm going to haunt you forever"

And even after I told it I did love it; it didn't believe me." Your lying Anna, I know you don't love me, Gramma told me so." " That's not true ." I screamed. " But it is." The doll laughed " She's here, she's always here, can't you see her or hear her, I can. She's right beside you." And she doesn't love you, she says you don't love her, that's why I keep coming back. And I'll keep returning till she's convinced you do love her. But that's never going to happen, because your nothing like her and don't appreciate the things she sent you. And you don't appreciate me."

But I do,"; I cried. But I knew it was to no avail, if Gramma was here, she was never going to believe me just like the doll. That's what I called it The Doll, I hated it so much I hadn't even bothered to

name it. And I was starting to hate
Gramma for the games she was playing
with me, and for sending the wretched
doll to me in the first place.

I had to get rid of both of them and get
rid of them fast, as I couldn't stand
anymore. But the question was how, and I
didn't have a clue how to go about it. I
couldn't exactly tell my parents they were
just as creepy as Gramma. My Mother had
even said there was something wrong
with me because I was nothing like
them.

But I knew there was something wrong
with them. But I couldn't prove it. I just
knew it was all just too weird. I felt like I
was trapped in a horror movie, A horror
movie that never ended.

Still, I had to either get out of here or
get rid of them and I was choosing to get
rid of Gramma and the doll, before they
got rid of me, because I knew if I didn't

that was what was going to happen, I would be the one to be replaced, or worse yet dead. And it was going to be the doll or a Gramma that caused it.

It was now or never, as I picked up the doll, I thought about how to do it. And suddenly I knew what to do I was going to tear it apart, as I started to pull its head off the doll started to laugh manically and sink its teeth into my throat, till then I didn't even know it had teeth. As I screamed it bit deeper, drawing pools of blood , blood that flowed profusely from my throat, as I realized I was dying. As I took my last breath, I heard Gramma's voice coming from the doll. " You should have loved me Anna, instead you hated me and now you're going to die."

3, The Teeth

As Elaine sat in the dentist chair and waited for Dr, Bentsen, she was really nervous, she hated dentists she had since childhood. And she hated the procedure she was having done today.

To say she was terrified of getting the implants put in was an understatement, she probably should have just gone with dentures, but Dr. Bentsen had talked her into the implants, a decision she was really regretting. As she knew it was going to be painful and a long healing process.
Something she was not looking forward too. Even though she was being put under, she was not happy about that either, as she waited on the Dr , she could feel her anxiety building. To the point she was about to throw up. As she fought the urge, she was glad, that it subsided, as she hated that feeling too.

" Well Elaine are we ready to begin? " , Dr. Bentsen said as he walked in." What's this we crap?"
she thought to herself, he isn't having anything done to him, he isn't being tortured. It's not his

mouth it's mine." Yes, I guess so." She almost whispered," Where is your assistant"" " Oh she will be here when I need her, all we are going to do right now is put you under so we can get started." As he head towards her with the anesthesia

 " I just want you to count backwards from a 100." As she started counting, she felt the mask being put over her face.Well it looked like it was too late to turn back now, there was no way she could change her mind now. As she felt herself getting groggy, she also felt the terror that was engulfing her.

   Something felt really strange, she wasn't sure what it was, or if it was even real. Strange sounds and visions raced through her mind, horrible sounds, and visions. Sounds of people screaming and they seemed to be covered in blood. Bright red blood. She tried to put her hands out to touch it, but to her horror her hands wouldn't move.

   Then she remembered where she was, that's right, she was getting implants, it couldn't be real, it was just a medication induced hallucination. Nothing more nothing

less, soon she would be awake, and the nightmare would be over. She would be back in control." Elaine, wake up, came the assistance voice, it's all over." As Elaine tried to open her eyes and respond, she couldn't believe how sleepy she still was. And the pain, in her mouth it was horrible, unbearable. As she reached her hands to touch her face it didn't feel real, everything was all rubbery.
" No dear we can't have you doing that, you don't want infection, now do you" " No." Elaine whispered the best she could, she could barely talk. Something was wrong terribly wrong. This wasn't how it was supposed to be.

Not only was she in extreme pain, but horrible visions also filled her mind . Visions of gruesome killings and the dead. People she did not know and had never seen. It had to be the medication, yet she knew it wasn't, it was something horrible more horrible than she could ever imagine.

What had the Dr. done to her, she tried to ask, but she was in too much pain to speak. It was all too crazy and unreal. As she thought about it, she suddenly realized how strange everyone had acted.

  As more nightmares entered her mind. She suddenly realized there were more to these implants that met the eye.

No wonder they were so cheap.

  Dr. Bentsen

4,Emma bird

Emma is a cockatiel that is owned by Cara Rogers, Emma seems very normal at first, but then strange things start happening and they are always in the middle of the night when Cara is sleeping, first there were just tiny scratches on her pale white skin. But it just got worse, in her dreams, Cara feels like something is pecking away and eating at her skin, something she chalks up to nightmares, but one night she wakes up and sees Emma sitting on her face, staring intently at her eye with her mouth open...

A vicious mouth ,a hungry mouth, a dangerous mouth. As Cara starts to scream a vicious little voice peeps at her" Scream all you wants Cara, no one is going to hear you it's only you and I." But female birds can't talk." Oh, but we can, we only chirp to throw you off track, you thought I couldn't get out of my cage, but you see I can."

" I've waited a long time for this, it's what you get for never letting me out of the cage." I begged and begged, and you ignored me, never noticing I was lonely. So now you're going to pay."

As Cara grabs Emma away from her face, the bird pecks at her viciously drawing blood everywhere she bit. As Cara grabs for her bird, Emma flies away out of her reach and hides among her porcelain dolls. But still watching Cara from her perch as she plans her next attack.

"I'm coming for you Cara ."Emma hissed from high up on her perch. I have plans for you, horrible painful plans. And I'm going to do it slowly. I can
 wait till your asleep again, you can't stay awake forever."

" Well, it's going to be long time till you can, I'm not the least bit sleepy." And neither am I .Chirped Emma. Well, you're going to be waiting a long time. Because I have no intention of going to sleep anytime soon you little bitch. Cara could feel her skin crawl as she thought of Emma pecking away at her, bit by bloody bit. She really wished she could catch her; she'd put her little butt back in the cage and this time she would put a lock on it.

   She had, had birds all her life and none of them had been like this. This bird was a bitch. A mean little bitch, plain and simple. And it wanted to kill her and was loose in the apartment, she was at its mercy. And though she had told Emma she could stay awake, she knew she couldn't, she was exhausted now and was about ready to pass out, but she had to stay awake, her life depended on it and besides she knew Emma couldn't stay awake either.

She had to fall asleep sometime. Cara just had to outlast her. Then she could catch her, it was just a matter of who could out last who. And she was determined it was going to be her, there were no ifs, ands I

or buts about it. She was going to outlast that bird and put her mean little ass back in the cage, then it was straight back to the pet shop where she had bought her. Then there would be no more birds it would just be her and her little dog Chewie .

But she could feel her eyes getting heavy as she thought about it, as Emma Bird attacked, she knew she had lost the battle as she took her last dying breath.

5. The fridge

My name is Muriel, and this is my story. Six months ago, I bought it , the haunted Fridge, as mine had broken. I couldn't believe my luck when I answered the old man's ad. It had merely said, used fridge $20:00 , you pick up , no deliveries.

Twenty bucks that was right up my alley and my budget. I couldn't go wrong. I was even lucky enough to borrow a truck and dolly from my friend Phil, I just hoped the old guy would be able to help me load it on the truck, I was strong, but not that strong.

Otherwise, I would be screwed and the whole deal would be off, and I would have to go to my local department store and order a new one and have it delivered. And there was no way I could afford that.

So, everything had to be perfect, if worse came to worse I would cry and wring my hands, men are suckers for that especially old ones. As I drove to the house, I really hoped luck would be with, me, I really needed this deal, and I needed the fridge.

   Though I could charge a new one it would put me in a deep dark hole finically. And I really didn't want to do that, I just hoped the old guy wouldn't be an ass and give any trouble. As I got closer, I started to get an uneasy feeling, but I shrugged off to meeting a stranger, I wasn't really good with strangers.

 Looking at addresses on the mailbox, I spotted the house quickly. And pulled into the driveway, it was a modest white wood framed house with black shutters, and it looked like the old man had lived here forever.

   The front door opened and a tall thin white haired old man who had to be at least 85 came out and motioned for me to follow him. Getting out I picked up my pace and followed him around the back of the house to an old workshop., that had seen better days. " " So, you're interested in my fridge missy, tell me what's your name, how old are you and what do you do?" Came the rush of questions. " My name is Muriel, I'm 26 years old and I'm a cashier at Sloan's Mini Mart. "

 " I see, so you need a good cheap fridge, cashiers don't make much money." " No, they don't Mr." " Just call me Jonesy, all my friends do." " Yes, I do Mr. Jonesy." " Before I sell you this deary I want you to know it's a very special fridge, I have had it for years, didn't plan on selling it, but medical expenses are getting to be right much"

 " I see I replied ." Trying my damndest to sound interested, when all I really wanted to do was get the fridge and get out of here, I was not known for my patience and I particularly didn't care for old people, they creeped me out."

" Well, here she is, I call her Mildred, after my late wife, God react her soul. " " I see." I replied still trying to sound interested. I hope I sounded believable, I did want Jonesy changing his mind, I really need the fridge, I sure as hell wasn't referring to her as Mildred, that wasn't happening, not in a week of Sundays. " Now you need to keep her set at 40 degrees at all times, we don't want nothing bad happening, now do we."

 " No sir" I mumbled. "You treat, Mildred right and she will treat you right. I want you to know before you buy her there are no refunds, if you're not satisfied." " I understand Jonesy, I'm sure the fridge will be just fine, it's just what I'm looking for."

 " Ok them missy, you've got a deal." As Jonesy muttered the words, I swore a strange kind of smile spread across his face," A smile that creeped me out more than he did. Hell, I just wanted to get out of here, I really hated old people's, especially creepy old men, old men that smelled and Jonesy smelled. Kind of like my great Grandfather George before he passed on, I hated that smell then and I hated it now.

"Would it be possible to get some help loading, it I really can't load it by myself." " No problem missy, I have my trusty dolly right here." Jonesy said as he loaded the fridge onto it and headed out the door towards my truck." I couldn't believe how agile he was and for and old guy, he was incredibly strong. I found myself wondering how, he kept himself in such great shape, to look at him you would have thought he wasn't as strong as a house fly.

" Do you need help, I asked." " Nah deary I've got it , old Mildred is just fine."

As he said that I thought I saw tears in his eyes. As I handed him the twenty-dollar bill, I shook his hand, and cringed, instead I

Of warm like mine, it wet, cold, and clammy. Suddenly I felt I really needed to get out of here and fast. " Well thank you Jonesy." I said, " I really appreciate it." " No problem ." Said Just remember there are no returns," As he spoke the words that same sort of smile crept across his lips.

   Quickly I got in the truck and turned the engine on and backed out, determined to get the hell outta there. As I drove home, I thought about his warning about the 40 degrees and knew there was no way I was going to do that everything would freeze up. A nice 60 degrees would do just fine. As I pulled in my driveway, I knew unloading the fridge wouldn't be easy, but

I had no choice, it was just me myself and I.

As I tugged on the fridge on the truck, I finally managed to get into onto the Dolly and headed towards the door with it, As I unlocked and the door, I steered it to the kitchen and set it in place and plugged it in and set it to 60 degrees. Well, that's a job done and done well if I say so myself, I thought, and better still, there was no Jonesy here to creep me the hell out.

It was just me my new fridge and my comfortable little house. I was as happy as a clam in salt water, getting myself a room temperature iced tea, I settled in for the evening, because it was now well past seven PM. Luckily, I wasn't hungry. Because I knew the fridge wouldn't be cold for hours.

As I settled in, I turned on the Tv and tried to watch a movie, that's when I first heard it a low moaning sound, almost like a woman crying. First it was a low muffled sound then it started to get louder, As I got up to investigate, I realized it was the fridge, oh great this can't be happening. Jonesy had said the fridge worked great, but now it sounded like it was on it last legs, but when I opened it, everything seemed fine, it was cold to the touch.

It was just making this weird moaning sound, though it was irritating, I figured it was something I could live with. So, I went back to my movie and settled back in, determined not to let it bother me. So, it had a weird quirk, as long as it worked besides what did I expect for twenty bucks. A brand new one.

Besides Jonesy said no returns and I had agreed to it. So, I was stuck with it, and it was stuck with me, when my movie ended, I didn't think any more about the sound and headed off to bed, I was off tomorrow and wanted to settle in. I hardly ever got a day off, being a cashier sucked, people were never happy, they were always bitching about something, they acted like I set the prices.

   As I slept , I started to hear a low breathing sound along with moaning, it was as if the house was alive, groggily I got out of bed and went I to the kitchen to investigate, the breathing was coming from everywhere and nowhere.
As looked at the fridge in the dark, my foot slipped on something cold and sticky, that hadn't been there earlier , I wondered what it was a
and turned on the light, to my horror it was a small puddle of bright red blood.

   As I tried to wrap my mind around it, the fridge let out
loud moaning sound that chilled me to the bone, chills ran down my spine, something wasn't right, there was no way this thing could be alive. But to my horror it was, as

I opened the door, I saw the most hideous thing I had ever seen, a pale white shriveled up arm and hand and a decaying head sitting next to it.

A head with dead vacant maggot filled eyes, staring, staring and wearing that same strange smile that Jonesy had. A smile that terrified me, I wanted to toss it all out, but I was too freaked out to touch it. Maybe I should call the police, but they would think I did it. As I backed away, I felt something on my shoulder, it was the dead hand and arm, wrapping itself around my throat, squeezing the life out of me, as I tried to scream it was futile, the hand had a death grip on me,

As it choked away my life force and I took my last dying breath , the last thing I heard was crazy laughter coming from the disemboweled head.

6,Dead fingers boney fingers

They hadn't been at the river very long,
when Janie decided to go swimming too,
though her friend Emily and her sister
Paula had advised against it . She could
remember Paula's exact words." Janie,
you don't want to go swimming in there,
there are weird things in there." "She's
right." Emily had hollered out." But I'd
course she hadn't listened; she just waded
right in and had paid no attention to Emily
or Paula.

As the warm water enveloped her, she
tried not to think about her sisters' words.
As they had been more of a warning than
an order. Awe Paula was just trying to
scare her and so was Emily. They were
always doing things like that, and she was
tired of it, she would show them and show
them good that there wasn't anything to
be afraid of.

She couldn't believe how good the water felt, yet there was something odd about it. That she couldn't quite figure out. There was a strange heaviness to it. She had never remembered it feeling like this, oh well it was probably nothing to worry about. So, it felt weird. " Janie you're out to far." Emily yelled. "You need to come back closer to shore." "Ok." She thought. " Sure, I do, you're just trying to ruin my fun as usual.", she yelled back." No really you do ." Her sister yelled" Your way out to far, bad things have happened here."

Yeah, she had heard that too, rumors had it that murders had occurred here, but that's all it was, was just some stinking rumors. And she wasn't about to let that stop her from swimming, she loved swimming and today was a hot day, brutally hot.

Hotter than usual, the heat index had to be over 100 she couldn't believe her sister and Emily hadn't come in too. She didn't know how they were standing it. As she swam, she felt something scrape against her leg, something strange.

As she tried to brush it off with her hand, it suddenly grabbed on to her hand and started tugging at it. Something slimy hard and yet something that felt dead, something that was trying to kill her, as she started screaming, she knew it was no use. She realized she was too far out to be heard and whatever this thing was it had a firm grip on her, a death grip.

How she wished she had not gone in and had listened to her sister and her friend ,but she had to be the showoff as usual and now she was screwed. There was no one to help her. Maybe if she dove under the water, she could see what it was and free herself. As she dove under, she tried to adjust her eyes to the murky water.

Thinking it was just a branch that had she had snagged her leg and hand on. But to her horror it was a Skelton that had grabbed her, with its dead boney fingers, fingers that weren't letting go. Fingers that were pulling her under and drowning her.

As she struggled to get air, she knew that the rumors had been right bad things did happen here and now they were happening to her. Somehow, she had to get help but to her horror she realized that Emily and her sister were nowhere in sight, they had disappeared, and she was all on her own.

If only she had listened, she would not be in the position she was now. Drowning with no hope of being saved, as she sank beneath the muddy water, she knew that

**she would just be another body the river
had claimed.**

7,The pothole

 As Stevie's car hit the huge pothole in the road, she cursed out loud." Damnit , and damn you wretched pothole, it's probably going to cost me a fortune to get my car realigned. I can't believe I hit that damn thing I was being so careful, but of course it was just my luck to hit it, nothing good ever happens to me, it's always something."

   Well, no use bitching about it anymore she thought as she headed home, the deed had been done and there wasn't anything she could do about it. As she pulled into her driveway, she had a very uneasy feeling, something wasn't right, but she couldn't place her finger on it. Maybe it would come to her later and she could figure it all out, at least she hoped she could, as she didn't like feeling this way.

As she unlocked and opened the car door, she was hit with the most vile and putrid smell, it was enough to make her sick, and as she stepped out of the car, her foot stepped into something gooey and sticky, she didn't remember that being there before, it was all so strange. She had never encountered anything like this, and she wasn't sure how to take it.

She didn't know what it all meant but she intended to find out, but till then she was going in the house and have a cold glass of iced tea with lemon, and a piece of her homemade coconut pie. She hadn't had lunch and she was hungry.

Tea and pie would hit the spot. But to her dismay when she went to open the door, the same sticky substance was on it as well. Someone had tried to get in her house, taking no chances she reached in her purse and took out her gun, after all she had a permit for it so she might as well use it. Opening the door as carefully as she could, trying the best she could not to get the substance on her, after all it could be anything. Poison for all she knew, she gingerly stepped inside and was assaulted by the smell vile smell

Putting her hand over her mouth she tried not to vomit, but it was too late, she threw up right where she was, great now she not only had to change she had to clean it up too and she had never been able to handle things like that, she would only get sicker, as she stumbled to her bedroom to change, she saw a trail of a black muscles like substance leading down the hall, . Well, this was just great too and even bigger mess to deal with." Damnit." She hissed under her breath," isn't this a bunch of crap, I can't believe this shit. This just isn't my day ." She screamed."

Like anyone could hear her or even gave a damn. Hell, she was completely alone, and she had been since Sam had left her a year ago saying he couldn't take anymore of her nonsense, it had just been her and the cat and that little bastard had runaway too. Now it was just her to deal with everything. No one even cared if she lived or died.

As she stepped around the black tarry mess, she made it to her bedroom and pulled off her rancid floor and tossed them into a pile on the floor. She needed a shower but, there was a trail leading to the bathroom as well,

It was like the goo was searching for something but what? There was nothing here, but her and that couldn't be it, that was utterly ridiculous , but then again you never could tell, about things. This hadn't exactly been the best of days. Well, she couldn't stand here nude, grabbing a pair of white Cotton panties from the drawer, she slipped them on and then put on the extra-large tee shirt, that she slept in from across the bed and put it on as well.

    After all no one was going to see her, so it really didn't matter what she had on. Though she was tired and just wanted to sink into the bed and sleep she knew she had the vomit to still deal with, so she headed towards the kitchen to get some cleaning supplies to clean it up.

    But as she stepped out of the door, she saw the mass had gotten bigger, " Damn ." She spat out, " this is all I need," Slowly she tried to step over it, but to her dismay, her right barefoot stepped it. " What the hell," she hollered as a strange burning sensation begin to pulse thru her. It felt as if her skin was being eaten by acid, as she looked at her foot in horror, she saw it turn the same color as the goo and start to inch up her leg till it got to her crotch.

Frantically she tried to wipe it away, but it was no use, the more she rubbed the more it spread over her. Dissolving every bit of skin, it touched. Mixing bits of flesh with the tarry substance.

Slowly devouring her soft delicate skin, as it reached her breast they to begin to dissolve and mix in with the gooey substance, she wanted to scream but it was already filling her mouth a nasal cavities. As she was consumed alive, the last thought in her mind was that if maybe she hadn't been such a bitch about everything, maybe she wouldn't be in the predicament she was in now, dying alone with no one to care, wether she lived or died.

8,The Ghost Walks at Midnight.

" Tess, have you heard the story of the ghost that walks at midnight?" " No Daniel, what is it? Tess asked. " Well, my uncle Jonah told me that if we go to old Flagg Road Cemetery ,we will see the ghost of old man Morris. And if we repeat, I don't believe, I don't believe, I don't believe three times that old man Morris's ghost will appear and lead us to his hidden treasure" .

" Do you think it's true Daniel?" " I don't know Tess, but I want to find out. " " Do you want to go with me?" " I don't know it sounds kind of creepy to me." " Of course, it's creepy Tess, we are going to a cemetery at Midnight. " "You mean you are going Daniel, I'm still not sure I want to do it."" You have to Tess; I've already told Uncle Jonah you were." " How could you do that, you know, that I get freaked out by creepy things.”

“ Well, I did so you have no choice now.” “ Well, I do, but I guess I can’t let you go there alone tonight. If we are going, we need to be prepared.” “ What do you mean prepared, how we need is just to go.”” No, we need flashlights , an EMF meter, warm clothes, because it’s supposed to be in the 20’s tonight. “

“ I guess you’re right ,” Daniel said as he went to get what they needed and to ask his uncle if they could use his ghost hunting equipment “ “ Well I got everything we need Tess, Uncle Jonas gave us the things we need to contact old man Morris. All he said was not to lose them. I told him we wouldn’t. Since it will be midnight soon, we need to head out.” Daniel said as he picked up the heavy duffle bag at his feet.”

" Yeah, I guess we had better, if we want to reach the cemetery at midnight." Tess said. With a quiver in her voice." You really are scared." Daniel laughed as he followed Tess to the car." Of course , I am. " Who wouldn't be, I mean normal people don't make a habit of being in a cemetery at midnight. I mean no one I know does, except you." As they got closer to the cemetery Anna could feel her skin prickle with dread of what laid ahead of them.

   Deep down she knew they shouldn't be doing this, it was just plain stupid, not to mention dangerous .She remembered the last person that had called old Mann Morris out at midnight, their torn shredded body had been found with nothing more than a dirty shovel in their cold dead hands. And a face that looked like it had seen the devil himself.

Tess knew she didn't want to be found like that. But she also knew that Daniel shouldn't attempt this by himself. Yet she also knew Daniel was not about to change his mind one little bit.

 Because money was his whole life. That's all he ever talked about, ever since his uncle had told him the story of old Man Morris. Tess could care less all she wanted was to get out of doing this. But that just wasn't going to happen.

 She was in for the long haul. " Well, we are here." Daniel said as the car came to a screeching halt." Time to call on old man Morris ." he laughed. "Yeah, right Daniel ." Tess said " Don't tell me your still afraid Tess. The dead can't hurt you only the living." Daniel called out as he rushed ahead to find old man Morris's grave." Thank a lot of Daniel ." Tess hollered as she tried to keep up." As she ran, she felt a stump catch her foot and down she went, face down in the soggy muddy grass.

As she struggled to get up, she found herself face to face with the old man's grave.

A grave that hadn't been kept up for years. A grave that she suddenly realized should not be disturbed, for now she knew that the story of the old man's treasure was nothing more than an old wife's tale.

As she heard Daniels screams in the distance, she knew that disturbing the dead had been a dangerous thing to do, as the horrified scream stopped.

She knew the Daniel was no longer part of the living.

"That's right missy, you're in the wrong place at the wrong time. And now it's time for you to pay the piper too " The old man said as he wrapped his boney fingers around her throat, and squeezed the very

**life out of her, as he dragged her into the
ground with him.**

9,Cracking Bones Deadly Bones

Anna Marie wasn't sure when it first started , she just knew that when her bones cracked, that bad things would happen.

It was almost as if they were speaking every time they cracked. " Anna, it won't be long till your dead, we want to kill you." Which was always followed by Crack! Crack! Crack! And pain like she had never known.

At first it had been only occasionally, but lately it had become constant . And now here she sat in Dr. Rawlings office waiting to be called . She wasn't even sure what she was going to say. I mean how does one, explain they were being attacked and talked to by their bones.

The whole thing was outrageous , she knew he would think she was crazy, and her next stop would be a visit to the county nut house as she liked to call it. No there had to be a better way to explain it. She just had to figure it out before they called her in . Instead of going into the truth she would just say she was in constant pain. Yea that's exactly what she would say.

   Then there would be no visit to the mad house, where they would treat her just like another crazy. She had heard rumors about that place, that once you were in there, it was almost impossible to get out. Well, there was no way she was going to let that happen.

 Her Mother had not raised a dumb child and stupid was not stamped across her forehead . ' " Anna Dr. Rawlings will see you now." Nurse Brightwater said, as she held the door open motioning for Anna to follow her.

As Anna got on the scale she wondered if the nurse could hear her bones cracking and whispering ." Anna, no one can help you, you're wasting your time being here." The voice laughed.

Anna watched to see if there was any change in the nurse's demeanor but there wasn't. " You're doing great Anna , you have lost fifteen more lbs. Since your last visit, the Dr .is going to be very pleased as should you." " As Anna shook her head, the voices hissed at her again , "That's because we are going to kill you. And there is nothing you can do to stop us or prevent it,"

Anna shuddered and tried to shake off the feeling of doom that she felt. She still couldn't believe that nurse Brightwater didn't hear it too.

Maybe she was crazy or it, was just a case of an overactive imagination and a crazy brain, working overtime. As she waited for the Dr, in the examination room, she still tried to get her thoughts together so she would sound coherent and not like a total basket case .

" Well, what brings you in today, Anna, it's been a while , since I have seen you." " I'm not sure, I'm just in a lot of pain lately. And my bones seem to be cracking and every time they do, I'm in more pain than I can bear. Can you give me something to help me? I can't stand it anymore ." " Anna there is no way your bones should be doing that . Your only twenty-five and what you are explaining usually only happens to people in their seventy's .

There has to be another reason for your pain." " I don't care what's causing it, I just want it to stop, you've got to make it stop, I can't stand it anymore more. Do you hear me make it stop already, or I'm going to a Dr, who will.",

" Calm down Anna that won't be necessary, I'm sure we can prescribe something that will help. You can take extra strength aspirin, right? " " Aspirin , you're only going to give me that. I'm telling you the pain is severe and you're just offering me that. I guess I'm going to have to go somewhere else ." " Anna, you know it's not our policy to prescribe pain meds. Unless it's serious like cancer and you do not have cancer.

I'm sure that aspirin will be just fine." " Well, I'm not, it's not your body and it's not your pain damn it! I came here for help and all you offer me is stinking aspirin .

I knew it would be useless to come here, I'll just take care of it myself." Anna said as she grabbed her purse and shoved past Dr. Rawlings, because she was pretty sure his next action was going to be to try and admit her to the nut house and that was just not happening today or any day for that matter.

   As Anna left the office, she could feel herself shake and her bones crack. And the crazy laughter of her tormentors . If she didn't get out of here fast, she knew that her next stop would be the mental Hospital , because she was sure they were being called right now.

   She had to get out of here now, before they arrived and forced her to go with them. As she started the car, she was pretty sure she heard the wailing of sirens. And if the cracking hissing bones weren't enough, she was suddenly experiencing sever itching in her left hand and arm.

   As started to check it out. She was alarmed to see a thick green pus, oozing down her arm, and oozing out of her hand.

   With an odor so foul she felt like she was going to retch any second. " No !" She screamed ." Damn you all to hell." She yelled as she tried to concentrate on driving." " ,Anna the voice's cackled as her bones cracked loudly, you are going to die Anna." "Stop I can't stand anymore ." Anna screamed ." You'd like that wouldn't you?" The bones laughed ." We are never going to stop until your dead Anna.":

   " There's got to be a way to stop them besides dying " Anna thought to herself. " I just have to figure it out." " There's got to be a way besides lousy Aspirin . What good is aspirin going to be?" Anna thought as she drove home.

   " Maybe I can make a deal, maybe there's something they really want that they aren't telling me." Anna thought as she continued to drive. " Is there something you want besides me dead?" She whispered .

   But the only reply she got was silence. " I can't believe I'm trying to make a deal with my own bones. I've got to be crazy to be thinking this way." " You are Anna." The bones taunted ."Crazy, Crazy, Crazy !" As pain shot thru her Anna could feel herself losing control of the car.

She knew that she couldn't stop the crash from happening and tried to brace herself for it. But she knew there was no way she could, as the sound of crunching and grinding metal filled her ears.

All she could do was hope that help was coming, but she knew it wasn't, there had been no one else on the highway but her. As the blood trickled into her eyes, she knew she was going to die here alone, while the voices taunted her unmercifully .' Crunch, crunch, crunch, ,die, die, die Anna they laughed as Anna struggled to breathe thru the gushing blood. Blood as hot and red as dying sunset. "It's ok Mam, don't struggle help is here. You're lucky we found you in the Knick of time. " The tall lanky paramedic said, as he help extract her from the mangled wreck. " They made me lose control." " They who Mam" " Why my bones of course. Didn't you hear them?" " I didn't hear anything, but you.   " They want to kill ; me they told me so." " Is that so?" Her rescuer said as he looked at her in disbelief. " George, we have a real case here." " She says she crashed because her bones are talking to her." " Sam, she must have hit her head hard in the crash. To be talking crazy like that. This one is headed straight to county general, then it's a quick transfer to the mental ward." " I know and she is a young one to, I'd say not much more than twenty-two or twenty-three." Sam replied. As they placed her into the ambulance, Anna Marie her eyes fill with tears as her chest got tighter and tighter . " Damn Sam do you hear that? It sounds like all of her

bones are breaking. I sure do, I've never heard anything like it."
 This one is going to be DOA for sure, hell I thought we got to her in time. But it doesn't look like we did. " George . As Anna's rib cage caved in, she knew the bones had done their evil dead as the sound of Crack! Crack! Crack! And the sounds of ominous laughter filled the ambulance, as the men closed her eyes and covered her with a clean white sheet. " Yeah, I really thought she was going to make, this just wasn't her day...Sam said. As he stared down at the cold dead body beside him." Yep, partner it just wasn't her day.

10,Nightmare From the Grave

Miranda knew she was at the right grave, a grave that was said to be haunted by the ghost of Robert Emery , a child that had been killed at the young age of seven in 1829 .

Rumors had it that he had been murdered by his stepfather Phillip, but it had never been proven. It was also said that Robert was a gentle spirit, And Miranda was determined to find out. Though she had been advised against visiting Robert's grave by the locals. She had decided to find out for herself, so here she was now, with nothing more than a flashlight, that worked when it wanted to.

" Robert are you there ? She whispered . But all she heard was silence dead silence. " Robert, do you have something you want to tell me?" She yelled. But once again all she got in response was silence.

" Oh hell, this is a bunch of crap, I'm really dumb to even believe this, much less try it. She said as she kicked the grave and turned to walk away.

" Yes, I'm here, and now you have to deal with me." Said a voice in the darkness. Miranda could feel her heart almost explode as she was grabbed and shoved to the ground. " You called me and now you have me"

As she tried to scream, only gurgling sounds omitted from her mouth. As she struggled to get to her feet. Ominous laughter surrounded her. Laughter that made her skin crawl.

As she got up, she started to run, but knew that she still wasn't alone, as the spirits hot breath enveloped her. Almost to the point of blinding her. " Run, all you want, but you will never be rid of me." Taunted the vengeful child's spirit. " Sweet my ass." She said as she ran towards her car, in the pitch blackness, with a flashlight that refused to work. As she got to her car, suddenly she felt alone . Alone in the cemetery that had no name. As she opened the door and got into the drivers' seat, she locked all the doors, just to be on the safe aside. " Well, that was a learning experience." She said aloud as she started up the car. " I hope whatever the hell it was, doesn't follow me."

But she knew that somehow it would. Still, she hope it wouldn't. How could she have been so dumb to visit a place she had been repeatedly warned about.

And had been dumb enough to visit armed with only an old worn-out flashlight . " Robert, I command you to go back to your grave." She whispered but the only reply was the dead silence again. Silence that unnerved just as much as the voice and laughter had. As she headed for home, she kept looking in her review mirror for some sign of the ghost she had encountered earlier . To her relief there was nothing there . " Miranda stop being ridiculous ." She said aloud " What you saw, was just the case of an overactive imagination. " Was it?" Came a small voice from the back seat. " I told you; you would never be rid of me." The voice hissed into her ear.

 " You should have listened to the warnings, but you didn't and look where it has landed you. " The disembodied voice said as it wrapped its icy fingers around her throat . " I was murdered and now you are going to be too. " Laughed the child. " As Miranda struggled to free herself from the unseen icy hands. She knew that her only chance of escape was to jump from the moving car and run for her life. As she opened the door, she threw herself out of the moving car.

Laying in the road, broken, and bleeding she watched as the car crashed and exploded into a fiery ball. "Smart move Miranda

." The unseen spirit laughed , as once again its icy cold fingers were around her throat again, squeezing the very life from her." " You should have listened Miranda .

" " I know." Miranda choked out as she took her last dying breath,

11,Uncle Ed's Topiary Cat

 Uncle Ed had been a gardener all his life and a cat lover as well. So, when his beloved cat Hernando passed away, he created a huge topiary image of it in his yard, which would have been fine, except he had become obsessed with it. Insisting it was indeed his beloved Hernando and was very much alive . And wanted him to see to its every need ,even if it meant no rest or sleep for the old man which disturbed his niece Margaret very much . She was even beginning to believe the giant topiary cat was alive too. Because she could swear, she heard it growling even in her sleep.

 Hernando has always been jealous of her and despised her and it appeared that the Topiary version of him did to. But that was crazy topiary cats were not alive and did not hiss or growl, or did they?

Margaret didn't Know but she needed to find out. Before it did the unthinkable to her and Uncle Ed. In fact, she even swore it was talking to her. " Margaret , I know you are glad

I died, I know you were always jealous of me and never liked me. And always wanted me gone. But I have come back and now you are going to be dead and gone too."

Yes, those were the words she had heard, and had tried to brush off as nothing more than a nightmare. But the words were real, and it wasn't a nightmare and Hernando was indeed back. But that was crazy too. Topiary Cats did, not hiss or growl and they certainly did not threaten and speak. But it was, and it had.

She had to find a way to destroy and be rid of it before it destroyed her and possibly Uncle ED too. But the question was how. Because uncle Ed was always guarding it and protecting it. He said he even knew what was happening with it in his sleep. And that in itself was crazy too. At least she thought it was, but things were so crazy she wasn't sure what was real, and what wasn't anymore.

 Maybe she should just pack up her stuff and leave and leave the business of the damn topiary cat to her crazy uncle Ed. Because she was convinced, he was indeed crazy. Because who would grow a giant topiary cat and insist it was alive and real if they weren't crazy.

 But she had the feeling that if she did pack up and leave the damn monstrosity of a cat would still find and do just as it had said it was going to do.

And kill her, she tried to erase that thought from her mind, but as a loud hissing growl, surrounded her she knew there would be no escape from the fate she knew awaited.

 As she struggled to escape, she felt the slash across the throat. And as the blood rushed out of her, the only sound she could make was a gurgling sound as she took her last breath.

Uncle Ed's Topiary Cat had done its job!

The Deadly crows

 The crow cocked its eye and stared at the pumpkin patch; something was coming he could feel it in the cool crisp air and smell it as well. He new it wouldn't be much longer till Halloween and the harvest of the dead began .
 He couldn't wait, the crows were already gathering, the old hallow tree was filled to the limit with crows waiting to begin the feast, a few more days and it would start, and they would fill their craws with the rotting flesh of the dead and when they were finished with them, the feast would begin on the living.
   A time of gorging and eating fresh flesh. And the first one he would feast on was Farmer Wilfred Davies himself. He had waited a long, long time, to give him his due.He had always been very cruel to them. Shooting at him and trying to poison him, not sharing his delicious corn.
 Now during the feast, revenge would be his. .Just three short hours and the carnage would begin. The crow couldn't wait, he intended to

be first to feast on the flesh and blood of Farmer Davies . As he thought about drool dripped from his beak and his beady eyes glowed a deep red, a red so dark, it looked like molten blood.

Farmer Davies stared out at the old oak and watched the crows. He had never seen so many crows in his life. There weren't enough bullets to kill them all, even the cemetery next was filled with them, as he watched them chills ran down his spine.

He knew something was going to happen and it wasn't going to be, good he could sense the evil they exuded . An evil he didn't like. As bad as he wished they were gone, he knew they weren't going anywhere, they were here to stay.

And so was he, he wasn't letting them get to him and he wasn't going out there with them. He wasn't stupid, He hated crows, always had since he was a boy. When he had been attacked by them on the way home.

The terror of that memory still haunted him torturing him in his dreams. As they pecked away at his flesh, flesh that ran red with blood.

Flesh that peeled away from his skin, dropping in putrid fleshy mounds on the ground, an attack in his dream that was so real he would awake from a sound sleep screaming, it was so bad he was terrified to go to sleep, and now the crows were here everywhere, cawing and hissing, and threatening to make his nightmares come true. He wanted them gone, he wanted them dead, but how, that was the question.
Even now he could hear them calling his name." Wilfred we are coming for you." We are going to devour your grisly bit by bit." Their threats shook him to the core.

   The crow watched eagerly he knew the the farmer could hear him and he knew that he was afraid, and that was how he wanted him to be. For the feast was now just a short hour away. First the dead and then the living. Wilfred would be his first victim; he had surveyed the house and knew the chimney was the quickest way in. So, the chimney it would be, and the first thing to go would be the Eyes, juicy little orbs of flesh a true delicious delicacy . They were his favorite and always left the victim helpless.

" Yes ." The old crow thought that was how it was going to be. An appetizer of a decaying corpse, then the farmers juicy orbits, and bits of his fresh flesh. He could hardly wait, it shook him to his core, he just wish the other crows hadn't thought about the old farmer, as he wouldn't be able to fight them off. And he wanted this delicacy to himself.

Farmer Davies, knew that whatever was going to happen, was going to be soon as the crows were getting noisier, and more agitated he could see them moving in and out of the trees. Though it was dark, he could make them out in is front porch light.

The constant cawing was driving him crazy and one particular crow was the worst. How he hated them and wanted them dead! " Damn it shut the hell up." He screamed, but it was to no avail, the screeching only got worse, and the one crow got even louder.

As he looked out towards the porch, he couldn't believe his eyes they were in a frenzy. There were crows everywhere and there was something hanging from their beaks, grisly things, to his horror he saw it was human. They were feasting on the dead from the cemetery next door. There were pieces of rotted flesh all over his porch.

   His gun he had to get to his gun, before it was too late, but to his horror it was already too late as the crow swooped down upon him and plucked out his eye and gulped it down.

   As blood trickled down his face. He knew his fate was sealed as thousands of crows began their attack upon him, ripping the flesh from his bones . As he took his last dying breath the last thing, he saw was the old crow on his chest staring him straight in the eye as it prepared to finish its feast.